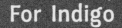

For Indigo

Henry Holt and Company, LLC
Publishers since 1866
175 Fifth Avenue
New York, New York 10010
www.henryholtkids.com

Henry Holt® is a registered trademark
of Henry Holt and Company, LLC.
Copyright © 2010 by Denise Fleming
All rights reserved.
Distributed in Canada by H. B. Fenn and Company Ltd.
Library of Congress Cataloging-in-Publication Data
Fleming, Denise.
Sleepy, oh so Sleepy / Denise Fleming.—1st ed.
p.   cm.
Summary: Depicts a number of animal babies sleeping
as a mother puts her own baby to bed.
ISBN 978-0-8050-8126-8
[1. Bedtime—Fiction. 2. Animals—Infancy—Fiction.
3. Mother and child—Fiction.] I. Title.
PZ7.F5994Sl 2010
[E]—dc22   2009006151

First Edition—2010
Printed in April 2010 in China by South China Printing Co. Ltd.,
Dongguan City, Guangdong Province, on acid-free paper. ∞

1   3   5   7   9   10   8   6   4   2

The illustrations are created by pulp painting, a papermaking technique using colored cotton fiber
poured through hand-cut stencils. Accents were added with pastel pencil.
Book design by Denise Fleming and David Powers.

Visit www.denisefleming.com.

Denise Fleming

Sleepy, oh so Sleepy

Henry Holt and Company • New York

Tiny baby panda,
sleepy, oh so sleepy.

Tiny baby ostrich,
sleepy, oh so sleepy.

Tiny baby lion,
sleepy, oh so sleepy.

Where's my sleepy baby?

Tiny baby penguin,
sleepy, oh so sleepy.

Tiny baby giraffe,

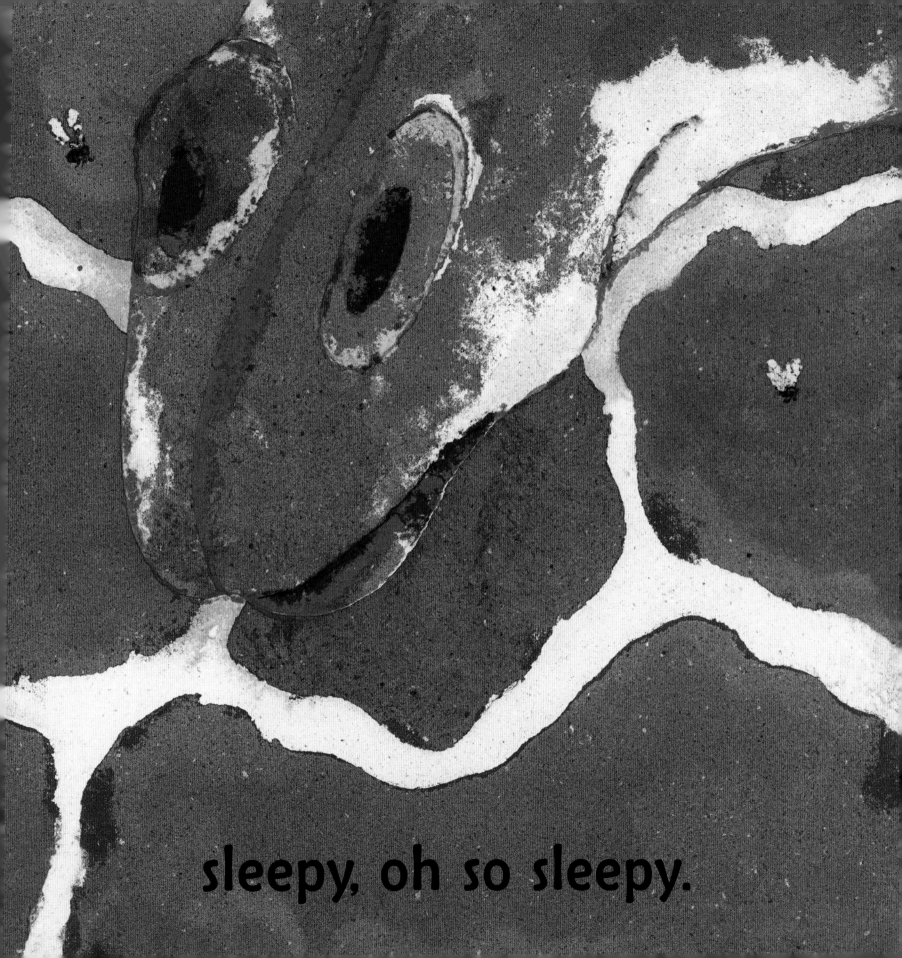

sleepy, oh so sleepy.

Tiny baby otter,
sleepy, oh so sleepy.

Where's my sleepy baby?

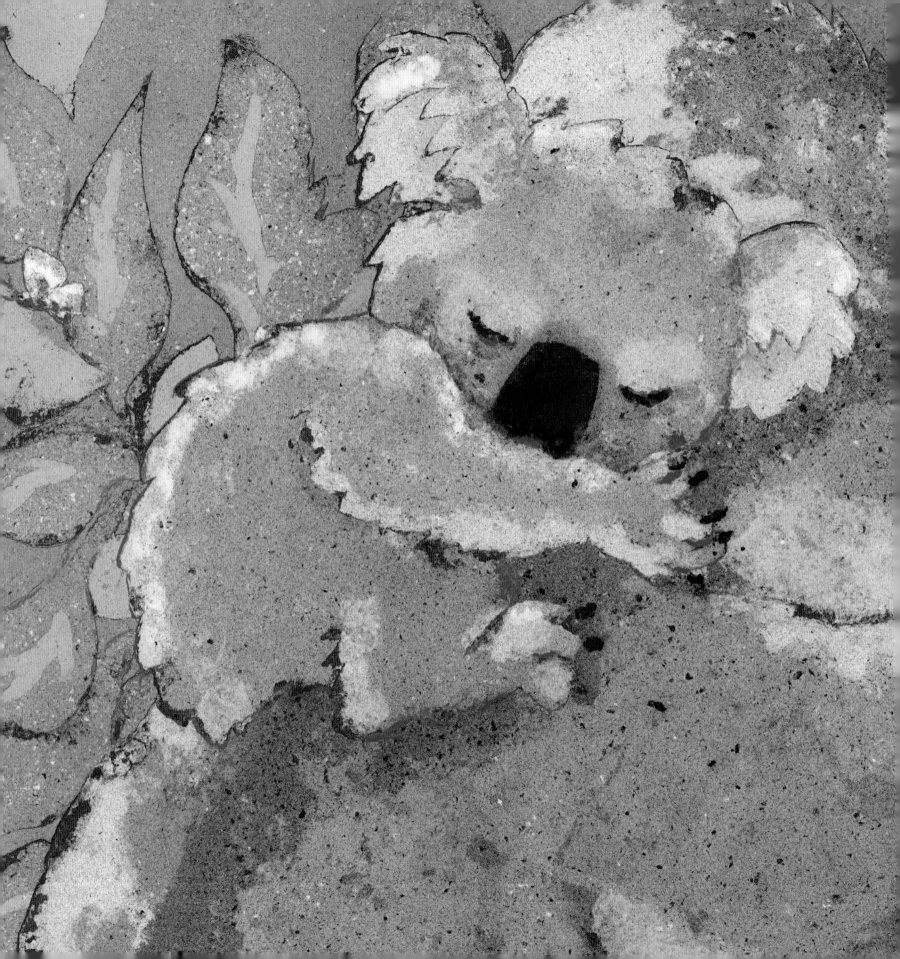

Tiny baby koala,
sleepy, oh so sleepy.

Tiny baby kangaroo,
sleepy, oh so sleepy.

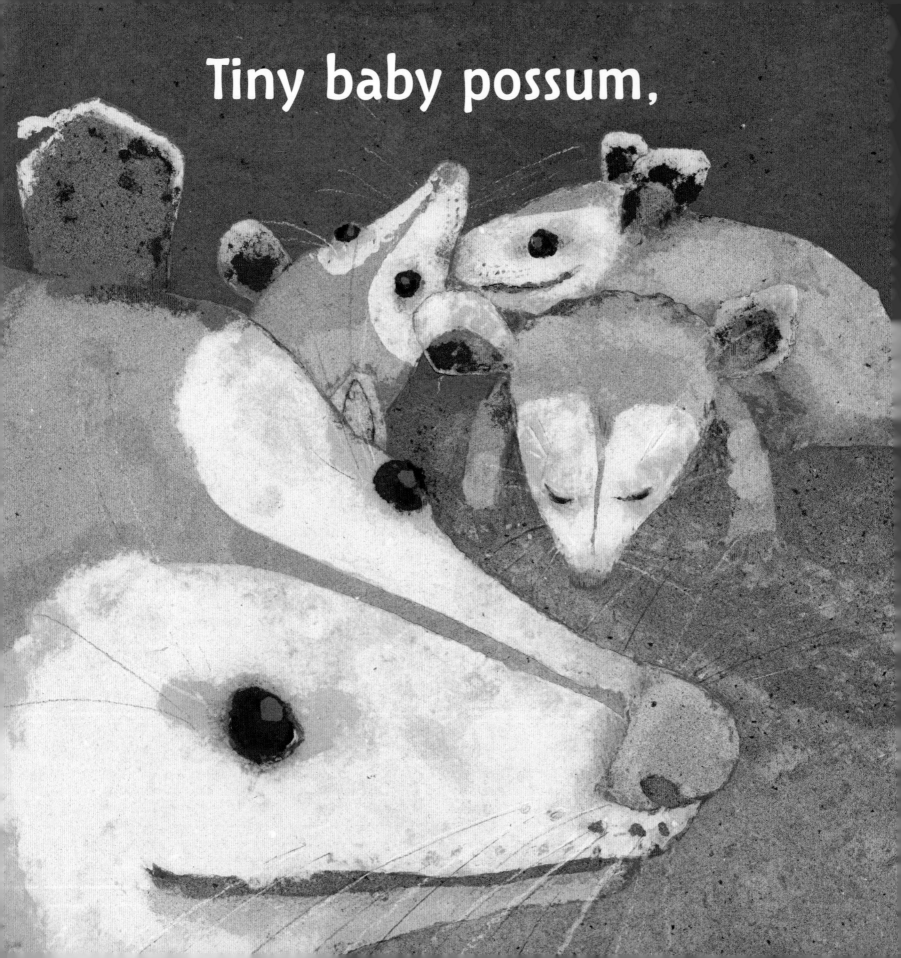

Tiny baby possum,

sleepy, oh so sleepy.

Where's my sleepy baby?

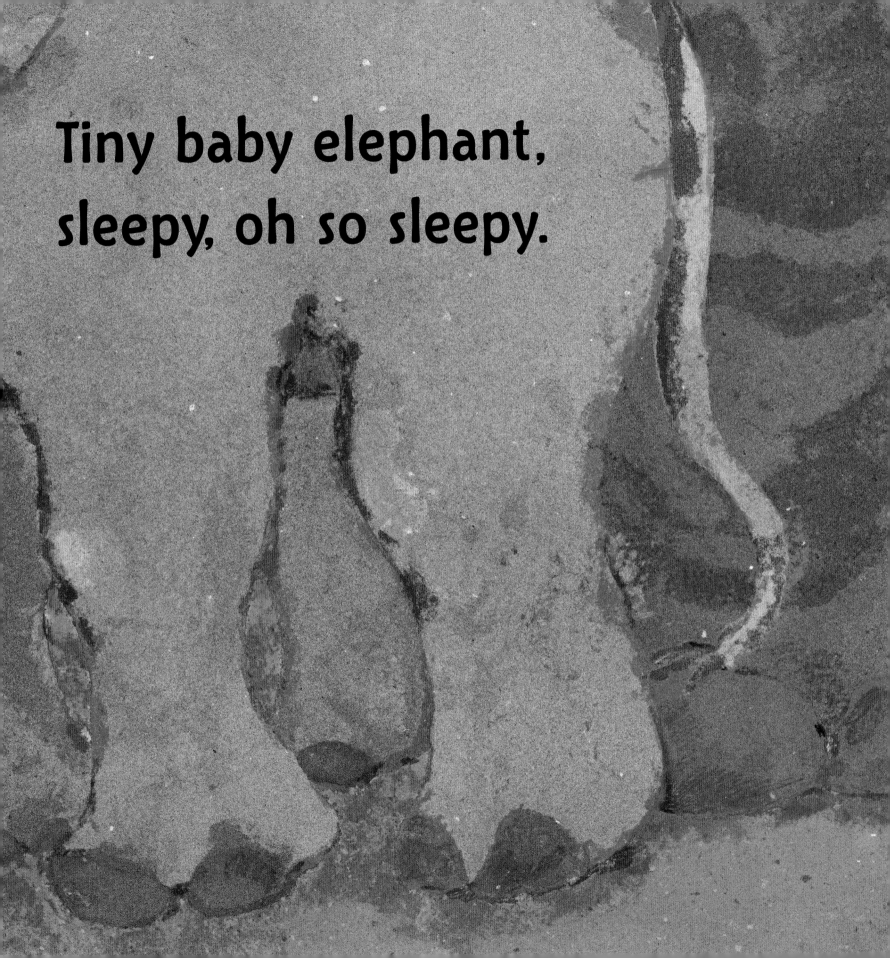

Tiny baby elephant,
sleepy, oh so sleepy.

Tiny baby anteater,
sleepy, oh so sleepy.

Tiny baby orangutan,
sleepy, oh so sleepy.

Where's my sleepy baby?

Here's my sleepy baby,

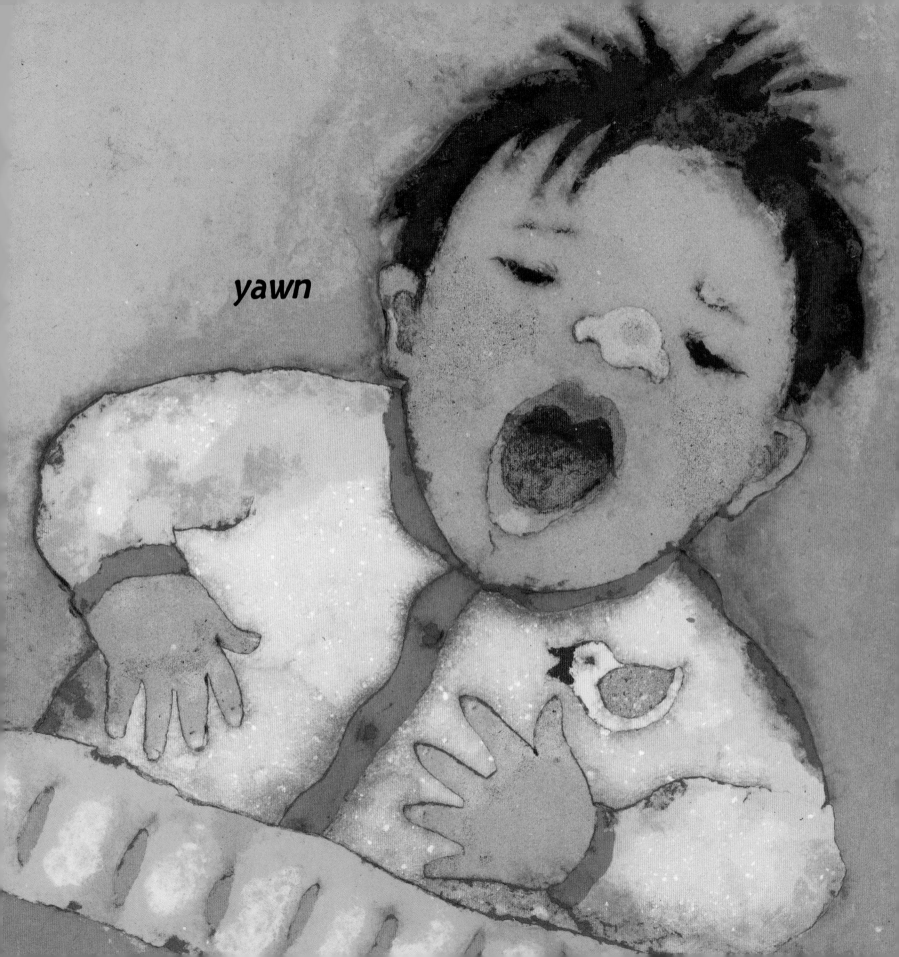

yawn

my tiny
sleepy baby.

Sleep tight, sleepy babies, tiny sleepy babies.